Fire Sale, Y'all

a trauma response
in poetry and prose

Kerry Lynne

Undashable Publishing LLC

ISBN: 979-8-218-51366-5

Library of Congress Control Number: 2024919709

This book is manufactured in the United States of America.

Copy editor: Janet Schwind
Cover design: Suzanne Parada

contents

note to reader 1

introduction 3

incipient 6

growth 23

fully developed 36

decay 65

letter to self 122

about the author 127

note to reader

Trigger Warning

This collection of stories and poems contains graphic and vivid depictions of sensitive and potentially distressing topics. It explores intense and challenging experiences that may be triggering for some individuals. Reader discretion is strongly advised.

Dialect

Some poems in this collection are written in dialect to reflect the cultural and regional influences that shaped my experiences and storytelling.

introduction

What is a fire sale?

Definition from Oxford English Dictionary:

FIRE SALE *noun*

: a sale of goods remaining after the destruction of commercial premises by fire

: a sale of goods or assets at a very low price, typically when the seller is facing bankruptcy.

For me, it was a trauma response. My marriage ended in betrayal. I was in a post-traumatic stress disorder (PTSD) episode lasting from the moment I learned the truth to likely months after the divorce was finalized.

Part of this PTSD episode included a deep feeling of claustrophobia. The marital residence and all its contents felt like a heavy anchor drowning me. I had to free myself of the burden somehow—and fast. I sold virtually everything in the house using a quick and efficient online auction and then sold the house. This is my definition of a Fire Sale, Y'all!

I offloaded things I needed.

I sold things I wanted.

I sold all the things.

I couldn't see past the moment I was in.

I was in crisis.

It didn't take long to realize I'd made a mistake. Fittingly, I have titled the chapters of this poetry collection based on the stages of fire development: Incipient, Growth, Fully Developed, and Decay (see Figure 1*).

In the incipient stage, you see how my childhood experiences and modeled family environment set the stage for dysfunction.

It's the growth stage where my own choices and state of mind are now in play, leading to a snowball effect as the fire rages to the flashover, which is the most intense growth point lending to the full development of the fire.

As the extent of betrayal is revealed, I make my way to the fully developed stage.

With time, the fire starts to die down and I regain control of my life as the embers of all the decisions I made in crisis now decay. The decay stage sounds terrible; however, it is in this phase where my healing occurs.

This is where I am now. In a state of acceptance and hopeful optimism. At least, most of the time.

Perhaps the fire sale had to happen to get me here. I no longer find myself in regret. I am understanding. Let me show you how I got here...

Kerry Lynne

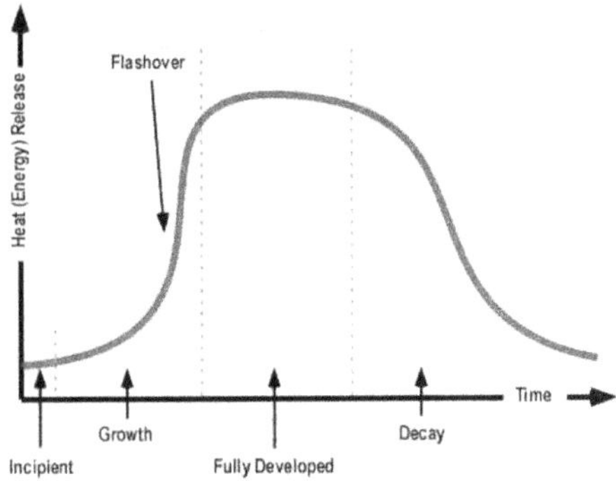

Figure 1: Fire Development

incipient

to me

This thing happened
A tragedy really
It happened to me
I mean, it was done
To me
Afterwards, I looked for help
I didn't find it

Alone
Truly
Those in my life
Who were supposed to help
Nurture
Protect
Did not happen
To me
I was young
Very young
Just how it was
So I thought this must be
How it is to be

Adapt
I went about my life
As best I could
Broken inside
From the thing
The doing thing
The done thing
Paralyzed inside
At times
Most times
I am good at alone
No one can hurt me again

When I am alone
It's safe

Doubt
All things
I stay busy
With doing things
Done things
Do more things
And so it goes
Choices present
I pass them by
By and by
It is nice
Staying still

Alone
Safe
Sometimes sad
I am sad
Sad doesn't hurt anymore
I know sad
It's always there
Like alone
Much time has passed
I am older
I'm wiser
I am strong but afraid
I feel weak but steady of hand
What do I have to show

Done things
Amount to nothing
Gone places
Nowhere is home
No one is my home

Nothing has happened
Since the thing was done

To me
No one belongs to me
I belong to no one
I am no one

set me free *(written in childhood)*

I remember being scared
Praying once again
It will be my mother to hold me and carry me home
The door opens, a man...
His face hidden by my own mind
I wrap the covers around me so tight
My fingers dig into my palm
His breath stinks of beer
His hands cold and rough
I begin to hate her more than he
For she was never there to set me free

bills and pills

Momma sits with puffed wet eyes, black from the night before
whoring
Only the pillow to wash her face
Not really
End of the month keeps coming
Every damn month but the money don't
The pills and the thrills ain't cheap either, but she ain't ever
gonna admit to that
A required numbing of the senses, no doubt
"Gotta roll the quarters and pinch the ends tight, girls
Stack the ones and count them twenties…
Man, this can't be right
Short again"
Long, hard sodomizing drag on the cigarette
"Don't scrub the stockings too hard, child, I have to wear 'em
this evening"
Tears staining her still perky breasts
Not perky enough to pay the bills
Damnit

remember

"Don't worry, he's here to help
Met him at the bar

He ain't gonna hurt us at all
Let's hurry and go before this one gets outta jail itching for
another soft face to bashup"

I touch my busted lip as she adjusts her collar over fresh purple
stained skin
I hadn't noticed it was purple until that moment, I remember
now

Feeling stronger that day though my lip wasn't right
I spat in his face this time

Hadn't ever done that to no one let alone a grown man chok-
ing my momma
Me and sis had to leave the kitties

I hated it, I remember still
Their soft cries

I cried too but not in front of nobody
Especially no stranger from a bar

Wasn't long before he put his hand in my shorts
I was the older one, still am of course

My boobs hadn't come in but he was squeezing them anyway
"Least he ain't hitting you, child

You remember that, okay?"
I never did forget, at least not about my kitties soft cries or his
hands, which never hit me

my nightmare

Sleeping on a concrete floor
Hearing cars pass, crack in the door

He's in bed, lying with mom
Hands on me when she ain't home

Catching the bus, front of the motel
Off to school, glad there's food there

Momma works, it's never enough
Strange men like to fuck or beat us

Will it get any better or maybe worse
Carrying around a trauma curse

I wake from a nightmare, has it passed
Face down, his hand pressed to my ass

No
I close my eyes and hold my breath again
What I wouldn't do for the strength to strangle him

I am weak as a kid, he strong as a man
I lay there praying for the day when I can

breath

I'll just hold my breath until I pass out. Then maybe I won't remember how this feels. Somehow I gasp for air despite my efforts. I am aware when he finishes and rolls off me. He snores now. His arm is just heavy enough I can't move. I shouldn't though, even if I could. I have nowhere to go. I just stare at the ceiling. There is a spider entangling something in her web. Something she plans to consume later. I wonder if the insect is numb like me or if it is just frozen in terror. I try to roll from under his arm and he drapes his leg across me. Maybe I will suffocate under his weight and this will finally be over. I hope he doesn't have another go before someone comes home. I may go completely mad. Have I gone completely mad already? Mom said he would help. She met him at the club and he couldn't wait to meet us. He had twisty curls and wore a zombie tee shirt with waterproof sandals...or at least the sandals announced "waterproof" on the side. A predator in sandals. A groomer. He told me he was habitually molested by his uncle as a boy. Should I blame the uncle? When I told mom he touched my backside she reminded me he wasn't hitting me, beating me. We had been through that. Nope, he never once hit me. Sometimes I wish he had instead.

brachial

How do you begin a story about seeing a man shot just after your thirteenth birthday? My new friends, who really didn't turn out to be friends at all, made blue koolaid with vodka in it. It tasted like shit but I drank it anyway. They thought I was weak. They were wrong. They played terrible music with the lights out and a boy put his hand up my shirt. It was his first time but not mine.

The next day I'm sitting outside warming my hands by a makeshift firepit in a stranger's backyard. We lived with that stranger. We were homeless, so we lived wherever we could. Next to me sat a demon. He had curly hair and a bald spot he tried to hide by leaving his hair long. He wasn't fooling anyone but himself.

Just then the stranger we lived with started yelling loudly from inside the house. I don't know what he said but the demon next to me seemed to understand. He jumped up from his seat, sending the decaying lawn chair tumbling back, and commanded me to get in the car. My mother always told me the demon had my best interest at heart. She was wrong, but in this case it seemed appropriate to listen and so I did what I was told and jumped into the passenger side just as the demon twisted the ignition.

The car stalled. It was ancient, so you really can't blame it. At that moment, I looked up to see the stranger, a very large but not as if fat, just a towering specimen of a man with his red face, swung open the screen door of his house with green mold growing on the vinyl siding. The screen door nearly flew off the hinges. He leaped over the porch stairs and came charging in our direction. The demon tried the ignition again and still nothing.

The stranger, to our amazement, did not come to the car. He stopped at a shed just in front of us and grabbed a sledgehammer. It looked like a regular hammer in his beastly hands. He stood at the front of the car, took a wide stance and swung the hammer up to the clouds behind his back and then down hard into the front of the car. The sound was magic. Metal pierced, folding in and screeching loudly, then a thudding to what I assumed was the engine.

The huge man, yet to let go of the hammer, attempted to dislodge it from the hood without success. My window was down. The demon opened the glovebox, his hand grazing my knee, sending shivers of familiar disgust up my spine. He was groping for something.

Before I could look up from the glovebox with its glinting revolver staring me down, the stranger was inside the window, the weight of him pressing me down deeper into the springs of the seat and his shoulder suffocating me as he wrestled with the demon. I heard a loud POP and felt warm liquid filling my pants.

To this day, I don't know for sure if I wet myself or if it was blood. The stranger recoiled from the car, dragging his bloody arm across my face. The bullet had hit his brachial artery. The blood tasted heavy and like nothing I had experienced before. I cannot describe it as there is nothing similar to which I am aware. I couldn't hear anything but a ringing.

The demon screamed at me and frantically touched my neck and stomach. I was unable to respond or move as my body seemed frozen in place. Not even disgust radiated my spine when he touched my breasts which hadn't really come in yet. Later, I realized he thought he may have shot me. He didn't. The stranger survived, but we couldn't live there anymore. It would be another 30 years before I actually saw a man die.

HELP his endless lies pulverize *(written in childhood)*

He will drag you to the wolves' den
He has slaughtered the alpha and plans to devour you
He reminds you endlessly, he is your savior
You don't want to believe him
But eventually you do

mary and judas

I am furious with you
You the chosen
You the brightest shining light
Not a blemish to your soul and not a scar on your face
My anger is likely misplaced
Who then made you
Should my scorn be placed at the feet of your maker
Our maker
I am touched by the darkness
I am peripheral to sin
The scars on my face and body a reminder of them
How can you look amongst your children and pick
"He will never be touched by sin"
"She will be plagued with darkness"
And then return to your clipboard, the mad scientist watch-
ing
What mother, what father would make this choice
How
Why
My womb bleeds
This damn apple
I don't believe it
Place women second and not in your image
The saddest joke of all, a rib, no more no less
From man's chest
Marginalized by words written by males
Males choosing from their superior placement in the light,
the goodness and the badness
Not within
Darkness done to them
They carry it around in their blackened hearts
Their blackened souls
Judas has a place

You decided he would be part of the blackened race
Where is he
Burning flesh
Or glowing light
I cannot bare the thought
Choosing a child to be dark
Then Mary, perched high and close to you
Never touched by sin
Did her womb bleed
Did she cry out in the night
How in the world
Why in the world would you choose a soul
To destroy, your golden foot stomping it into the soil
I am furious with you
Dammit
Dammit
Answer me!

thriving neglect (nasturtium flower)

My first memory was of a towering black figure with dark, empty eyes. He tousled the prairie grass and found me hiding. My mother didn't notice as he carried me away in his clutches.

He was fast as the wind and the prairie was a blur long before the sun set. He stopped, tired from the journey. As he rested, his grip on me loosened and I was knocked from his grasp, tumbling down and down onto the soft wet ground. It was dark and he gave up the search for me rather quickly.

I didn't know where I was, the dew on the grass was sweet and the moonlight settled me in for a great long and dark nap. I was there for some time. I couldn't tell you how many days may have passed. I focused on gathering my strength as I knew a very important day was coming.

Then, the day came. I wanted out of my refuge. I needed out. The time was now. I struggled against the dirt that settled on my back and finally reached up and up and up until I was sliced and pushed down. I recoiled. Never taking in the sun. I rest again, gathering my strength.

Days passed, maybe months. Was it a year? How sleepy I had become. I had lost count. Surviving on water and whatever the earth provided within my reach each day. I was stronger now.

Once again, I burst forth with power and vigor and the greatest desire for the sun to touch my face. And there it was. The glorious sun. He warmed my face and I stretched as far as I could to take in the fullness of his grace within me but the briar pricked and sliced me again. This time I did not waiver. I looked around to see the space I was given and I dominated it.

The briar protected me when the sun was too much to bear, keeping me from withering. We learned to live together. I thrived among the greenbriar. One day the towering crow returned, his eyes deep with knowing me even in my glorious powerful form.

He declared my kind survived best in harsh and neglectful habitats. I had saved for him the sweetest dew in my petals and as he drank, I whispered for him to take my seed up and away to another corner of the world and he did just that.

As I turned to watch him go, the briar ripped and scratched my face. It was no matter—he was capable and amiable to the task and my seed would thrive wherever the crow flies.

what you did

Is there someone in your life who either did horrible things to you or more passively allowed horrible things to happen to you? Then the person grows and becomes kinder, wiser and more tolerant, almost like a completely different person. Then, for whatever reason, this past misdeed is discussed and somehow they are now traumatized at the weight of what they did from this new perspective they have and you find yourself consoling them for the abuses you endured at their neglect? It's completely fucked!

growth

the whispering ghost

SHhhh
Do you see them
The ghosts

Traded a lifetime
For a moment
Of darkness

Careful
Their disease is contagious
Don't let them inside

It will consume you
The thought
Of trading a lifetime
For a moment

It's a plague
The darkness
Needs more
To swallow
The light

Never dull your spark
Don't trade a lifetime
For a moment
In the dark

reflection

Line my eyes
Line my lips
Glittered perfume
Staining my hips

Pushing buttons
On a board
DJ is blindingly bored

Two parts water
Three parts Jack
Powdered nose
Water back

Pasties on my nipples
Rubbing raw
5-inch heels
Make me feel small

Sweat pants
Bitch dance

20 down
20 more
What am I paying you for
You dirty whore

Mirrored reflection
Girl, aged 3
Where a grown woman
Dances seductively

love

Legendary
To be beautiful
It needs to be tragic
In lies the magic

Love
Crashing like a truck
Breezing like the wind
Where is the magic
Is it tragic

How
How do we go on
Putting the show on
It is fragile
Hard to handle

When
When the curtain is closing
The crowd overflowing
Lights are showing
It's tragic
Lost the magic

End
Confetti in the hallway
Popcorn on the seats
Mascara dripping doorways
It is tragic
It is magic

juxtaposition

Juxtaposition of her light
In the shadows I delight

Love so sweet
It burns my skin
Makes me want
To sin again

Soft kisses of goodbye
Gotta work late
Another lie

Her smile unknowing
My dark deeds
Never revealing
Carnal need

Weighs on me
She loving blindly
My cowardice
Beckons forcibly

I must speak it
This, my sin
Make the burden
Smaller then

She spreads her wings
I think to fly away
Instead she shelters me
From the fray

She is more
Than I can bare
To my whore

I am snare

Me, the sinner
Her, no saint
Love will never
Satiate

trained

Come one
Come all
What a sight to see
And this one here
Trained by me

Not me alone
I cannot claim
She was once broken
All the same

She perches there
Just as I shout
Sit up straight
Don't fuss about

She does not bite
She does not kick
With a pet she may just lick

What a joy it has been
Breaking this one cleanly in

Pride, I have to share with you
Though boring now, her subdued

Another toy I must collect
Conditioning of all defect

As behaved as she can be
I do not wish to set her free

Collecting them may be a chore
But having just one is such a bore

Oh so pretty she would be
With another trained by me

mmm hmm mmm

Been hearing all kinda things 'bout you
Heard yo man ain't happy
Been diddling the waitress
That local cafe

She put the scones in a box for me
Smiling ear to ear
While banging your husband
In the parking lot rear
Hope the skank wash her hands

'Fore she brewing the mayor's coffee
Heard he skimming dollars
From the park fund
That new Tesla ain't cost him none
Damn potholes ain't fixin 'emselves

Heard the teller ye old apothecary
Splitting pills for his worry
He is high as a kite
Mixing the meds
Nothing coming out right
Since who knows when

Huh? What, what ya heard 'bout me
Sitting front the library
Spewing up stories?
Well no, all I says da truth
What ya needing
Some kinda proof
Mmm hmm mmm
Done heard dat 'bout you

just lay there

"Why can't you just lay there and let me fuck you"

She remembers he said
And she did just that
Laid there and wished she were dead

This isn't a false story
This isn't fiction

This is something a husband said to his wife
All the while screwing someone else in his double life

To this day these words are still in her head
But no longer does she wish she were dead

Instead she moved on and picked things up
Now she simply hopes he truly gets fucked

taken

You can't take the taken
Try as you may
If love is there
No dismay

Pile on the makeup
Stick out your ass
Whip your hair
As he pass

You will never be
As virtuous as me
To anyone
Especially he

So make a show
Embarrassing all others
You, the joke at home
We tell each other

If a partnered man should fall
For your foolish advances
He was never taken at all
Deserves nothing more
Your painted smile and fake eyelashes

don't laugh

I don't like the way you laugh
The way you dress
The way you smile

I don't like you
You recluse
You bore

You just happened to be the best option at the time
17 years ago
Not now, though

Not a while back either
But I didn't tell you about that neither

You found out on your own
The truth, I denied and continued to hide
It's easier to blame you for the sickness I have inside

You are gone now
I wasn't expecting you to leave so quickly but it's a relief really

I wouldn't touch you when you cried because of my lies
And I still don't like the way you laugh

believe

Why do I doubt my...
Beauty
Worth
Value
Importance
Intelligence
Prowess
Experience
Why do I doubt myself
My beauty will never fail as it was grown in pain and suffering
My value has been paid in heavenly blood and can never be
tainted by anyone, even myself
I am loyal, honest, and faithful to a fault which is not a fault
It is to be celebrated
I deserve celebration
My intelligence grows by the day and my desire to learn is
unceasing
I don't need anyone or anything to prove any of this
The breath in my lungs is proof enough
I must simply believe
Believe

fully developed

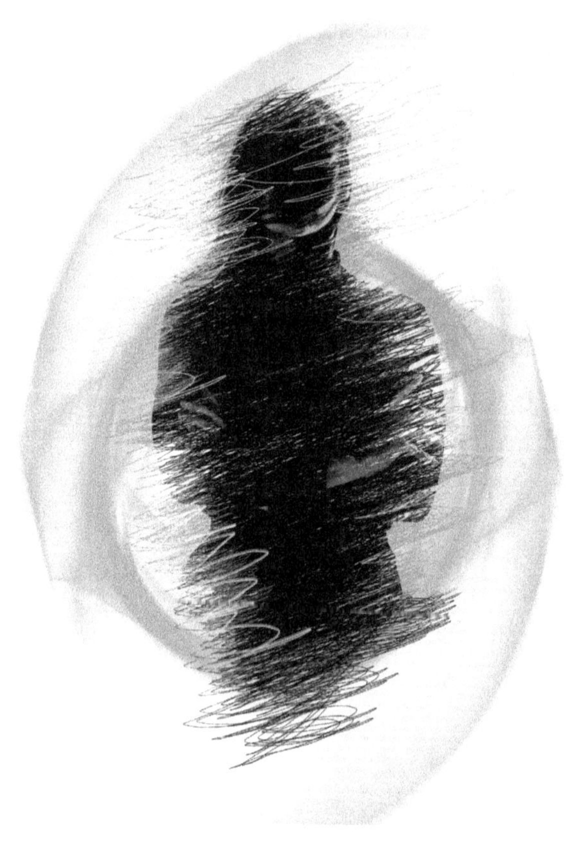

fuck you

Shake your cold finger right in my face
Turn up your lip, nose in haste
Treat me like a child
Whatever it takes to make yourself feel worthwhile
I'm taking notes here in my head
Holding the cards of doubt and dread
You are a cold heart
A calloused shell
Fuck you
Fuck you
Can't believe I ever fucked you
You little shit for a man
Not worth the turd on my shoe
Kick you off but the smell lingers
My mind has to be the most incredible thing
Strong as diamonds and metal
Made this bastard of a man look capable
I have always seen the best in people
Possibilities and worth
Forgiveness a strength, I thought at first
Now I'm certain of this great strength but understand the
power it holds
Pray now to see the real thing
The person, not just the original mold
See people for who they are
The vision of what they could be, should be, a great power
Only to those who deserve, will I allow
Where there is good, there is bad
That's what I wished I had
Before you yelled and belittled me
Now it's your ghost, the real you, that haunts me
The power it has is only power if I give it
So on this day I squash it

Like that stinky turd under my shoe
Fuck you
Fuck you
I washed my shoe and your stench is exorcised
Goodbye, you disgusting piece of shit

scarlet letter

I do not envy her, though she left her mark on you. That was something I never got to do. Despite all the time we had. There it was—bright copper tone orange, front and center on your chest. What is she, maybe 5'2"? Painted on face and hair as black as a L'Oreal Starry Night and dry as October field corn decorating your arm. She was crying. What would I have you do? You had the nerve to say. A woman you have known for a few months gets to rest her powdery face on your chest and I your wife am left crying untouched in a closet while you stare at me. Enjoy the marriage bed you have soiled with her incontinence. I will leave you with a scarlet letter. Rather than an "A" I will choose "F-U."

lion's share

Does he wake you sleeping deep
With that gasping stutter
My darling

His dreams are of himself
In case you haven't
Figured it out yet

No need to worry about me
Not that I'd ever come back
He won't step back, either
He believes himself too clever

All his mistakes are on the backs of others
Ready yourself for the lion's share
My darling

Check the shadows
Check the bank statements
Check his phone

Check yourself
At the door
There is no room for you
Anymore

His ego needs the lion's share
Take care
My darling

paper mache

Why are you sitting there with that smug look on your face
As if it was you who put me in this place
What a relief for someone else to share your house of cards
I'll be far, far away building something real, it's my charge
You and your lies are like paper mache
A simple gust of air and they blew away
The only person ever capable of fooling me
Has always been and will always be...me

loneliness

The sun is resting down below
The moon reflects its ghostly glow

Alone I sit but yet again
Struggling the demon within
Its teeth it bares daringly
Beckoning and calling me

It bites my flesh and pulls my hair
I'm never free of this snare
All the pain for which I tangle
Leaves me bare, broken, mangled

Loneliness

How am I to overcome
All of which has made me numb
Are these feelings even real
I cannot trust what I feel

I have been fooled so many times
Never one to tow the line
Am I to repair the seam
When I feel this is a dream

All is good but will it last
I recall this too shall pass

time

Gasping for air as I turn the corner. My pace quickens and my breath follows. My legs will surely give out before I am free of his grasp. Yet I still run. Harder and faster than ever before. The wind is at my back, I will surely make it through this time. He cannot force his will anymore. There's a field ahead, my refuge. I dart suddenly into rows of corn as the sun ducks behind the clouds. I drop to my knees and clap my hands together in silent prayer. Please, God, won't you spare me, save me, do not allow him to ensnare me. He devours me from the inside, please keep me safe, Lord. Won't you please…The sun escapes the clouds and shines brightly on my trembling face. My eyes are tightly shut. I hear his steps. He is massive. The corn bends to his will and he towers over me. With his calloused hand he lifts my face, now wet with tears. I shiver and give in to his demand to rise and kiss him passionately.

He is TIME and I have nothing without him.

wolf

Eyes on fire
Both warning and desire

The growl reverberates
My heartbeat hastes

He approaches snarling
To the entry come clawing

His drool, silver mercury
In the moonlight
I cannot escape
The still of night

Insatiable appetite
I pray the gate holds
Keeping me safe
From more than the cold

I lean against the door
Cage of brick and mortar
Falling slowly to the floor
His cries of thunder

The rhythmic bane
Lulls me to sleep
Numbness now
As I weep

I awake in horror
To see him there
Nose in my stomach
Blood stained air

He looks inquisitively
I reach to push away
My hand so weak
On his head it lay

He rests alongside me
We dream together
He lives on
Death I surrender

moment

Crawling to the bathroom
The pills they work too well
Sleeping my escape
Momentary hell
Only the dreams
Aren't a reprieve
All that you deceive
Clawing at me
As I sleep
Weeping
Wet

blasphemous

On my knees with head in my shaking hands. I know You may not like to hear this again. Please understand, You may have made a huge mistake. I'm not supposed to be here. My legs are strong but my heart is weak. My stomach is iron but my shoulders are deficit. The dead weigh heavily on me. The living a megaton more. The carelessness of the world is toxic. My blood is running slower by the day. Throbbing head from bleeding saline eyes. Promise me to look at Your notes again. I'm certain I am supposed to be in a place of comfort, kindness a culture. Serenity and understanding, the way of life. Where all of man are of equal value in your eyes and all others. I cannot belong here. The burden is unbearable. Brief moments of love are hardly enough to sustain the poor and meek. Please won't You look again?

My greatest and most powerful Lord, I remain Your servant. All my love, the suffering.

the glimpse

Who are you

The one who wakes up alone and knows the number of steps
to the toilet
Like a zombie you stumble to relieve yourself, wanting noth-
ing more than to get back to sleep
Being awake is exhausting

Or
The one who wakes up unsure if you're alone with no idea
where you are
Frantically scratching at the walls to find a light switch that
doesn't exist
It's not safe to go back to sleep, am I asleep, nothing is safe

Maybe
The one who wakes up next to someone wondering who this
person really is
Can you ever really know anyone
Ever

Besides, who are you, lying there questioning another when
you have no idea who you are, even with all the perspective of
your existence

You can never know who someone else is
Never, ever

You lucky ones may someday get a glimpse of who you are

If it doesn't scare you, then you aren't really being honest with
yourself

mirage

Trembling
Relentless tears staining my best coat
Cold
Mud on my suede boots
Wondering
When I cry real tears over a mirage life does it make it real
Decide
The tears are real, my feelings are real but it doesn't make
anything true
Forgiveness
To myself for my unpreparedness when I am defined as such
Defining
A new self, alone, but with the greatest hope and desire for a
true partner
Real
I am real, my feelings are real, I was truly there
Goodbye
Dissipating mirage and hello to something painstakingly real,
I hope

do you see

When you wake in the night
With cold aching in your shoulders
A woman lies next to you
The moon revealing shadows upon her face
What do you see

The life she has created or the life she has silenced
The lines of her face revealing richness, joy or the lines of
sorrow, defeat
Her mouth, the fullness of pleasure it implores or the thin
razor with words c u t t i n g
Her neck, its proud height steadfast with the family's success
or it folding, her chin to chest unable to carry the hopes of her
kin
Her bosom a playground of softness or hollow cavern of
grieving heart
What do you see

If you see her
You see it all

guns from the south

He prolly shoulda told ya
Bless your mascara-dripping heart
I don't mess around
Ain't no pretending here
You shit in my front yard
It's time you see
How Kentucky girls get hard

Calling up the family
From Lexington to Appalachia
These guns from the south
Gonna get cha, get cha, get cha

Won't none of it
Ever come on back to me
Only thing colder than
My guns from the south
Is the dirt where your
Spray-tanned face gon' be

cum and shit

Ladies are to be kind and sweet
Make him dinner and rub his feet
Suck his dick
Take his shit
With a smile

Well, I heard you are what you eat
I have been eating dick
And swallowing shit
So, I am not a lady

I'm a crazed madwoman full of cum and shit
You will make space for me or I will throw up
All the shit I've been fed right in your eye
Stand in my way
I dare you
Oh
I **double** dare you

pyro

I am one inappropriate glance
One misplaced word
Away from burning
Everything down

Don't ask for a smile
Don't tell me I am pretty
Don't tell me I am ugly
Stop TELLING me a damn thing

What is your problem
I know what mine is
You and others like you
And not enough matches

dark and twisted

You are fucked in the head
Dark and twisted
What has happened to you
You are crazy
Total basket case

Thank you kindly
For putting me in my place
I know darkness
I know fear
I know evil
And it's all right here

Once you've experienced it
Even at another's hand
It won't leave you
I don't believe it can

It marinates
It dwells
It festers

I write of mine
It pours out of me
I have no choice

Or maybe I do
What if I didn't share it
What if I held it all inside

The poison will have its day
I truly think it's better this way

Let it be words on a page
Instead of deeds performed

So fuck off, you perfect boring losers
I have some dark and twisted shit to write

If I don't write I might cut you into little pieces
So, ha ha yep, run away you cowardly bitches

fuck luck

I am here
Waiting in line
With all the other mindless
Humans

Where is my share of the blame
Shame
Perhaps fame
If I sell my soul
The bidding is low

Place your bid
Buyer's premium is 10 percent

Fuck
A blow job and fucking is
$100 on Figueroa
Ruining my life
Is currently at $8.00
Midwest hoes bargain

Problem is
I think I'm too good
For sex work
But give it for free
Drunk twerk

Sold my life
And all I had
$11k so I could
Live in an apartment and play

Vibrator is always charged
But I had maxed out all my cards

Men are simple
Men are easy
Paying the bills with my
Tits ain't sleazy
Right

Wrong
I don't fucking know
My genetics keep drowning me
I'm two seconds from selling me
Always

You wanna fuck
I'm down on my luck

shadows

I lost my joy
I lost my faith
I am stuck in this shadow place
I don't know how I got here
I don't know how to get out
I don't know what this sadness is even about
Drowning in tiredness
I have slept all day
I cannot eat
I cannot go
I must stay
No thoughts make sense
But they won't subside
I withdraw
From all I should hide
The shadow consumes
My head is pounding
Or is someone at the door
Please go away
I have nothing left to say
Don't make me explain
Don't make me eat
Let me lie here in the shadow of my defeat
If you must stay then come inside
From everyone else I must hide
In the shadow with you isn't the worst
Careful though, contagious may be my curse

our baby

I chewed the bitter pills
They made me weak
Then finally sleep

You were there
Vinyl chair
Hand to my stomach
Gotta do this
Baby's coming
What is her name
You looked the same

Until you held her
That was love
Not for me
But for her

Spilled milk
Sleep came easy
Never the time
Lullaby rhymes
Balloons on the mailbox
Pink and purple
Still not for me
But for her

Absent from the table
There when you're able
No time for family
Not me or her
But this other
As it were

I wake from the dream
Cold chills
And scream
You never loved me
Hardly hugged me
Thank God you did her
Please just love her
Do you still love her

I pray it's true
You love her
And not just
Yourself

54 percent

Fifty-four percent
I was awarded
50/50 state
Seemingly a win
What of the sin

Blemished with failure
His and mine
Was I a prude
Was I a stiff
Was I a bitch

Was he always going to cheat
Was there anything else
It never should have been
He was never good enough
For me

I just didn't know my value yet
Looking at myself like the dollar menu
I am the prized pig
Settled for liver
When I should of had ribs

Now I know my value
Now I have my half
Plus four percent of his
I get to take my pick

I pick me
Oh...and some of that
And that
And that too
OH, that...

dream

There's nothing here for me
I'm long long gone
But you, dearest
Will cry out alone
At dawn

I am crushing
Like the waves of the ocean
Pulling you in
And pushing away
No sense, baby
I'm trying to go my way

And I will
You will be left
Unfulfilled

Dream those dreams
My fingertips combing your hair
My tongue caressing you there

Dreams take my place
Waking in a cold sweat
Hot head, gone baby
Cannot replace

I held your hopes
You withheld
Your darkness
So dream your dreams—
Of me, as if you will ever
Have me again, never

dubious

She called
Bedroom eyes in the photo
He saved to his phone
Ring, ring, there she is
Beckoning him
Beckoning our child, though we didn't know it right away
Beckoning me, eventually
I answered for too long
They broke up
She was sorry
I thought she was sorry for what they did
I think she was sorry they broke up
I listened despite my utter confusion
It seemed like the right thing to do
Until the third breakup
The third phone call
She told me he was trying
Trying to do what
I had no idea and still don't
Why was she sticking up for him
She was sorry again
I don't think she was EVER sorry
Now she makes my daughter dinner
She sits on my old couch with him
They watch football on our old TV
Or at least they sit next to each other
Escaping in their phones while pretending
To watch TV with my daughter sitting there
What are they sorry about
They aren't sorry
She doesn't call me anymore
My therapist told me not to answer
Being Christian didn't require the level of kindness I was

offering
To my husband's whore
She isn't his whore anymore
We are divorced
She is his roommate
She cooks and cleans
She does my daughter's laundry
Cuts her hair and buys her makeup
I wanted to strangle her for a time
Now, I want to thank her for saving me from mediocrity
It's a dubious thing
They aren't sorry
I'm not sorry either
The gratefulness I have for these two abounds
My loss, 17 years
My gain, a beautiful daughter and another 17 years or more
of exactly the kind of life I desire
Without the narcissistic husband
Without the basket-case whore
What glorious thing should I do today!?

decay

brunch

Arriving forestall to ladies brunch, positioning myself as the solvent of our motley brood...

All the while my torn sock disobediently slipping into the heel of my shoe.

Can I not be a formidable heroine? Who of you be the tale-bearer of my counterfeit husband? How can you be so trifle as the whites of my eyes are still red with the truth of his deeds? Wait, but I am the trifle who doth gossip on and on and much about my own discretions. What a monger I be but if only to control the pain of the story...

I soften my jaw and smile at each wondrous beauty, jubilant in this eclectic mix of friends growing more boisterous as each hen arrives!

Much affection is bestowed on me as they have grown to understand how great a need I have for such petting. Do they see me as a toddler over the formidable heroine for which my armor betrays? Not a care I give, I pretend. I do much adore the way I smell after embracing each of them.

Sea salt, is it? With vanilla, gardenia, coconut, perhaps white tea all mixing with my own lilac oils in an intoxicating explosion of fragrance I simply cannot recreate despite my continued efforts to do just that. Neither bakery nor bouquet renders close to this euphoria of scent. My plight continues...

The harlots speak of the pleasures and pains of courtship in the modern world. What is a girl to do? Does not our hardest grain of rice in the softest wet and sacred garden of our deepest treasure deserve exploring? Exploration by our own labors, of course, is a work of mastery...but why not share in the engineering of the project? The struggle to find a foreman with existing acumen or the desire to learn is tiresome. We digress...

Those with mates speak mostly fairer truths. I know these woes. Boring, settled, uncompromising partners... But what do I know? Perhaps all is well, or so they believe, as I did. I beg that all is well. My foreman was fired long ago. He became overwhelmed with multiple projects employing his tools all around town, using my credit to pay for these lavish builds! "The gluttonous bastard" they all sing in unison! You don't know what you don't know, until you know. Silently, I pray my brood be forever spared of the deep crushing void in my heart. A void I yearn to satisfy, but fear will never be bursting again.

I've ascertained all relationships are rife with unknowing. Speaking of which...I take in a deep breath and listen intently to the tales of my harlots. These imperfectly splendorous women are the most fascinating of creatures I have ever had the pleasure of smelling.

mind the gap

Thank you
You who met me where I was
You who said I was enough
The one who held me when I was crazy with wet cheeks
You who listened when I didn't make sense
You who prayed when I couldn't speak
The one who loved me when I was vulnerable and still when
I was a conqueror
You who stepped aside when my boldness grew
You who stepped up when I had nothing left to prove
The one standing there in the gap
Thank you

nerve

You got some kind of nerve
The greatest liar I have ever known
Doesn't trust me

Then a momentary pause
Look at how special I am
The greatest actress he has ever known

The lioness he poked in the dark
I am awake, he is the mark

Damn straight
Lock up your gates
Build up your walls
No man is ever too tall
To be struck down
By the greatest monster of all

A woman scorned
By a man so small

birthing

He came to me
Like in a dream
Flirting round the couch
Smell a smoke
Stuck in the textile

The ad said OBO
Black and white ink
Staining fingertips
He bought the sofa
But stole my light
I didn't put up
Much of a fight

Funny thing happens when
A man leaves you with nothing
You quickly manifest
Rebirthing everything

Birthing is the
Woman's greatest gift
We will always be
Better off than the fate
That is his

The man always seems to forget
The woman is his
Greatest gift

better

Twist the knife
Pick the scab
Nothing left of what I had

Say the words
Eat the pain
Never want to feel ashamed

Hard to know
What is real
Just need time to let it heal

One step forward
Two steps back
I will run when I feel trapped

Push it down
On the inside
Nowhere left for me to hide

I can't trust
Not a one
What is this I have become

Then I wonder
Will it ever
Please oh God make it better

purge

There stands a single erect hundred year old sycamore along the riverbed. The carcasses of her ancestors swallowed by the river's unforgiving flow. A country road hugs the river too closely and ends abruptly at a gas station. On the lowest branch of her outstretched arms, the sycamore holds a single leaf. The leaf is yellow and brown, like an overripe banana. The leaf trembles in the late November wind, desperately holding to the sycamore. Just below the trembling leaf is a gaping hole. Festering the sycamore from the inside out. The hole is black and bulging along the edges. In the black hole's line of sight stands a woman pumping gas at the station. Her hair whipping her cheeks wildly as the cool wind meets the warm clinging to the surface of the earth. She is crying. She is crying hard. People pass the crying woman painstakingly pretending not to notice her shoulders shaking uncontrollably as she succumbs to the purge of saline cleansing horrors from her mind. The woman welcomes the wind tangling her hair, blinding her from the strangers hurrying along as if the world isn't ending. Once the purge is complete the gas handle clicks, the woman wipes her face with her hands, replaces the handle, takes a deep breath and returns to the road ahead. The sycamore releases her last leaf as the wind from the woman's car stirs up purging within her own branches. The leaf tumbles madly in the wind until kissing the surface of the river where it is swallowed, never to be seen again.

vessel

Who is there
I say to you
You have bound me
With your traditions
Wrapped in robes
Of gold leaf
Sipping holy wine
Flesh on your chin
While the baby cries
Momma's impotent breast

Who is it
I beg
Has bound me
With this ring
Solid gold
Chastised
While he tomcats
About town
Not a sheath
For protection

What is this
I tremble
No foothold
Newness of
The charge I have
Now blistering
My lips parched
Ready for the
Chalice of life

Bring.it.on

little big men

You fuck us before our periods come
Looking for a child to tame

Then pound us again as we bleed
A little more careful with your aim

You take our light then run away
You bare your teeth and clench your fist
As if you are stronger
You are so weak minded
You little big men

We have been broken and beaten
Fucked and mistreated
Say we stay in our place
Goddamn paint to hide our face
Hide the scars from tears
Flowing riverbed

I say no
I will not sit quietly
I will not dress nicely
I will not do as I am told
I am not the fairer sex
I am the brightest bold

I am strong as a diamond
The pressure I have endured
I break metal with my glance
Do not take the chance
Of cutting me down again

I will fucking destroy you
We will fucking destroy you
I am woman
I am women

I am big
I am little
I am strong
I am weak
I am the sex you will
Never defeat

bitch

I think I have a bitch inside
One that is no longer okay to hide
She wants to come out
To scream and moan
Can't complain that she feels alone
The nice girl has been in charge for too long
She plays the long game and prefers to be home
The bitch wants to run and play and binge
Its about time to shut the nice girl in
I am damn tired
I am damn weak
I want to be strong
I want to freak
I want what I want and I fucking deserve it
I don't, but don't you worry 'bout it
Mind your business and sit back
Can't you see I am on the attack
It is my time
So just sit down
Give me space
Or stick around
I just may show my tits

path

There is a hole, a great divide
You stand there on the other side
Holding out your hand above the abyss
As if I must jump to you from this
I look around and see a path
But then you start to shake and laugh
Do I not understand this game
Now I'm overcome with shame
Should I jump into the darkness
With its gaping open starkness
The path beside me is comforting
Is there something there unseen
How am I supposed to know
Exactly which way I should go

this is the place

Here is where the faceless man ripped my nightgown
Here is where the boy plunged the screwdriver inside me
Here is where I peed my pants
Here is where he kicked me when I was down
Here is where I spit in his face
Here is where my virginity was taken
Here is where I saw the man shot
Here is where my child was murdered
Here is where I walked barefoot in the snow
Here is where the pavement bruised my face
Here is where I saw Jesus
Here is where I learned the truth
Here is where I ran away
Here is where I started over
Here is where I wrote it all down
Here is where I choose to be

veil

I know God, Jesus is my friend
Catholic is where my journey began

Trapped inside, unsavory bond
Left him with his mistress forlorn

Priest sat quietly, mulling MY sin
Filthy marriage bed I'm to stay in

Take the wine, they call blood
Problem is I know the flesh
Had the blood, smelled the stench

Taste of iron, not of wine
Feeling different, crossed the line

Say I can't leave, or need permission
Court church, my admission

Tell the dirty secrets
A man in black
Says hold nothing back

I already prayed, I already confessed
Jesus loves me, no less

The man takes notes, purses his lips
Shakes my hand, lovely quip

Cry in the car, say a prayer
Release me from this, tangled layer

Sign of the cross, cement I'm lost
But not from God, not from Jesus
From this veil, you beseech us

No religion can ever trample
A love for Jesus this ample

within

The greatest war to ever win
Is the one you fight within
Do not weary in battle
Sharpen the mind
Bludgeon the heart
Do not falter at the sight
Blood and shadows
A day is not enough
Introspection to endeavor
A lifetime to toil
Treasure found
Lost again
The battle is never won
Within
You must begin
Again and again
Found a moment
Fleeting and clever
Chase it once more
Twice, thrice
Then as you breath
Your dying breath
No need to prepare
Your authentic self
Spent your life
Unearthing
Living and beginning
Embrace the ending

find yourself

You have to find yourself
Before you can fix yourself

Start at the beginning
As far as you know
No need to relive the trauma
Be delicate as you go

Look among the rubble
There are glimpses of you
Of course to survive
You became someone new

If you look hard
Search very deep
You are there
Just asleep

Find the hints
Sprinkled all around
Take them up
Feet on the ground

Put them back
The pieces of you
Accept them all
Be renewed

You have to find yourself
Before you can free yourself

lost and found

When a lost thing is found it becomes the finder's
Finders are often careless with a free thing they find
Theft by finding, no doubt the heart of a thief is no heart at
all
When a found thing is found it may accept or decline the
founder's invitation
Founders understand the value of a found thing and will treat
it as such
Founders have a heart to grow found things
If lost, hurry along the finding of yourself
It will be your greatest investment
Be found, whatever you are

the snitch

I see you
Begging for attention in that photo
Though pretending to be passive
In the situation and details
Hard to drive past the train wreck
Without craning your long rubbery neck
You will not slow me down
Go, tell your tales
Tell them as whispery
Or as loud as you want
I am preparing to sing
Sing mine from the very highest
Black and white mountain
Of burning ash
Snitches are often forgotten
But a narrated story of disaster
In first person, of course
Will always leave a dark spot
Folks remember

impolite

Being tolerant of the intolerant is a matter of utter exhaustion
Truly, a work of marionette masturbation
The audacity
In this crazy world I live in, however
This is the predicament I am in
Mindless people vomiting hateful spew at complete strangers
Or worse, passive aggressive dismissive behaviors meant to
beat me down in the most polite way
Pretending to be Christians
Excuse me while I fix the smile on my face and leave
You do not deserve another moment of my precious time
Good day

switching sides

Now that you are here
Snooping around the debris
Listening to my wailing
Watching the videos of me weep
Don't get any grand ideas
I'd sooner skin you
And salt your hide
Then let you come on over
To the other side

called to do

It seems more often I am crossing paths with people like you
Each time I pause and remind myself what I am called to do
I forgive you
For kicking me when I was down
For throwing your weight all around
For being cold and patronizing
Such great efforts to clip my wings
For putting me right there in my place
Not a care to save some face
Taking your whole pound of flesh
Leaving me there with nothing left
The night falls and the lonely suffer
Off to bed without so much as supper
In the morning though, I know what to do
I rise up and say a prayer for you
You are forgiven too

here all night

Ain't nothing wrong
Things just don't seem right
My chest warms wet cheeks
Tear stained skin
It's comfort she seeks
Her breath slows to mine
Slumber overtakes
I'm resolved for all time
"I'll be here all night, if you need me"
I whisper
Baby

best parts

My heart is such a small place to grow
But that is where you started
I prayed
I begged
And you appeared there
The tiniest of ideas
You outgrew the space rather quickly
Settling inside my belly with a seed
This seed helped you be more than just a prayer or an idea
You existed
Floating in a delicate space that wasn't too delicate at least for
a while
You turned and twisted your way to the sound of my voice
You liked the vacuum but not burritos
I imagined your face
Your cries
But nothing in my wildest dreams came close to the magnifi-
cence that is you
That first day and every day that passes is filled with such
discovery of the abundance of majesty you are
Oddly enough, you like burritos but not the vacuum 12 years
later
Your eyes are the same color
Your hair lightened by the sun
You are so much more than me and the seed
You are the best parts
Thank you for loving me

ionized blue

There be a lady
Where a child once stood
Her hair in tangled tendrils
Eyes blazing ionized blue
Heart racing with tiny feet
Graceful now, her legs long
As the stem of the sunflower
Turning brown in the sun
Her hair bleached
The same sun
Kisses her
As I did, in the mourn
And as we say a prayer
She falls to slumber in my arms
As she stands with brown legs
Her hand still outstretched
Begging for mine
Her eyes still an ionized blue
There she be
A lady
Hardly a baby
But holding my hand
All the same

play, sing, never give up

Oils from her lovely fingers massaging black and white keys
She is the best at intoxicating me
Voice is soft and textured like the prairie grass
Play some more is all I ask
Write the songs or just the notes
I'll help you with the final quotes
If you want
All I want
Is for you to play
Play, child
Play

Door should be closed
Doesn't want anyone to know
How she can glow in her flow
Then she needs help with a line
Or maybe how to work the time
Momma, help me with the right word
To make this song I wrote superb
It's perfect, baby
But I'm so glad you asked
Sing it to me and we'll nail it at last
Goosebumps at how her mind works
The notes come out and her voice within
Sing it to me baby, again and again
If you want
All I want
Is for you to sing
Sing, child
Sing

Should I slide my voice right here
Or draw the air deeper there
Nasal maybe or should it be throaty

Let me hear then, show me
Writing a song with an angel
Voice like a prairie and face a meadow
Together we build this thing of hers
Bridge by bridge and verse by verse
She lets me in to help perfect
A creation in her dialect
Mind and body
Verse and sound
Our creative minds
Forever bound
No matter the day
No matter the things
Promise me to always play and always sing
If you want
All I want
Is for you to never give up
Never give up, child
Never give up

breathing

Why am I crying
I'm crying because breathing hurts
The oxygen burns
I have been deprived of air for so very long
I have been strangled by my family, by my men, by myself for
most of my life
For the first time
I am breathing and it hurts
It really hurts
And I couldn't be more exhilarated by the experience

my name

What's in a name? For some: money, fame, royalty, lineage, politics.
For others, everything...literally all their meaning is from the name. Tragedy.
Nothing is in my name.
No hillbilly will hear my name and know we are the same with the rusted tires on cinders in the front and back patch a mud.
No redneck hears my name and revs the diesel for me though we shared a neighborly fence.
The black women don't know me from Adam though we climbed the same tree and pulled 'dads from the same crook.
The poor white girls don't remember how we stuffed our bras in gym class.
Even still, the rich white women don't know me either. Though we wear the same skirt at $1K. Hers just dry cleaned and mine rented.
No one knows my name. It means nothing though I AM everything. I AM all things and no thing, everything.
I am free.

mutiny

Why do you still lie to me
In black and white the county doth decree
If we are honest the ties never bound you anyway
So perplexed why you still lie today
Old lies, sure, gotta maintain the facade
But these new ones feel rather odd
Suddenly it occurs to me
Perhaps your lies were never about me
You lie for yourself for reasons unknown
I'll not interfere with this path you are on
Fooling yourself is a skill I am rather equipped
I'll sit idly as you sink, mutiny your ship

ignorance isn't bliss

What is this of the new way
I rather liked the old
Or at least, in the ignorance
I believed it so
NO, what a silly thought
Once the boat has set sail
There isn't a turning to port
How could you
Now that you have the knowing
And if I am honest
Ignorance wasn't bliss
It was settling
For I knew nothing
Of the new
Or even the old
Okay, so let me admit this
Many things keep me
Rolling in linen
The darkest hours
My only and youngest
Sharing her with a stranger
Who I settled with for more
Than I care to recall
This I would surely prefer
Be more like the old
Stroking her hair as
Sun come up
Clasping her hand
Prayer as it go down
I rather liked the old
Though, only of her
However, I say surely
Loving a facade

A heartless man
NO, I would not choose
The old, not ever again
I shall never be okay
With ignorance
Not ever

undashable

You need to stop hitching your wagon to these men, she said.
Oh my, I thought, how the kettle does scream when it is good
and hot.
She has 20 years on me, the rest of 'em I was bouncing on her
hip or not far behind her ass which I seem to have inherited...
I soften my eyes and ask momma what she means.
You wanted a big family, he changed his mind and took that
away. Painful reminder my child bearing years are gone...(I
clench my jaw) as consolation you asked to adopt, he said no
again, maybe host a student from Guatemala for a year and
still he said no.
Blessed with one beautiful grand baby from you though, she
winks. I melt and laugh.
Damn, this brilliantly flawed woman has such a hold on me.
You had other dreams along the way, she continued, but
somehow someone always stopped you.
Daughter, it's time you took control and had dreams no man,
no person, can ever dash. You need undashable dreams. Set
them now and start pulling your own wagon. Shit! She's
right. And so began my list of undashable dreams.

momma says

Momma says
There is no need for me to worry
She will remember he had a girlfriend in a hurry
How weak I was
And then how strong
And likely how we didn't get along
At least there at the end
When you stopped pretending it was all me
Yelling and screaming like a banshee
The money you spent
I won't get back
She will remember all we lacked
As I picked up the pieces
Made a new life work
While you stood there smugly
Your uniform a smirk
I didn't sleep
Processing your lies
With my brokenness on the inside
How her and I found ways to grow
In ways you will never know
All the time her and I spent alone
You with a girlfriend already in your home
Me a single mom
You the absent dad
It'll be too late
When you remember what you had
Momma says her and I will be okay
Up ahead are better days

broken and better

My daughter broke her favorite piggy bank. She was so very sad. Her beautiful hurt face swollen and red. We collected all the pieces, big and small and put them on the counter. She felt careless and irresponsible for how she handled something so precious to her. We talked about buying a new one, but nothing would ever be as good as this one, she declared. Can you fix it, mommy? Please, can we try? She begged. I told her we could, but it was so broken it wouldn't be the same. It would have cracks and scars everywhere. She smiled her biggest and most authentic smile and said it didn't matter to her if it wasn't perfect. And so, we fixed it. We glued every piece in place and wrapped it with rubber bands hoping to set it together like the weak puzzle it had now become. The next day I removed the bands and wouldn't you know, it held together! With its dozens of scars big and small, it held together. I felt it needed a bandaid across its behind to finish off the new look and was skeptical she would still want it, given its obvious state of disrepair. She was ecstatic. She delicately took it from my hands, touched the bandaid and smiled. She loved it, and it was even better than it had been before it was broken, she assured me. She placed it back in its spot and patted its head. This was several years ago. She still has the piggy bank and today I recalled this memory...I missed her, as I often do now that I have her only half the time. I went to her room and lay in her bed seeing the piggy bank perched on a shelf. There I lay among her things, broken but better than I have ever been, thanks to her teaching, I finally understood that.

thank you

The first day I met you I knew I was supposed to. I could feel that. I didn't know what it meant then but I feel as though I am figuring it out now. I was meant to burn to ash and be reborn again with the knowledge of what I wanted after not having it for so very long. You held the match. And you used it. You used it so well. I have crawled out of the ash. I was completely broken. But I healed and now I am stronger in the broken places. The best parts of me that embarrassed you and the worst parts of me that you tried to manipulate away are all still here. However, something incredible has happened. I have nursed those wounds and embraced who I am. I am shining brighter. Even more brightly than before that fateful day you walked into my life. I am brighter, weirder, sexier, and more sure of who I am today. As each day passes I grow stronger. Strong enough to fall with eyes-wide-open in love with someone. I will not change a single thing about who I am for anyone ever again, thanks to you. I will be loved for my laugh with the occasional snort. I will be loved for my service to others even in the most awkward of moments. I will be loved for my natural beauty. I will be loved for all the things that make me weak and all the things that make me strong. I will be loved.

colored past

Born in Kentucky
Daddy spot empty
A blue certificate
Still haunts me

Momma left me
Then came back
Before adoption
Had a red stamp

Yellow car
Wouldn't start
Blood was red
My pounding heart

Baby's name
Was River
Never a chance
To deliver
Not a color
I remember

Whitest dress
Others burgundy
Promised to always
Stay true to me

Older than most
Momma made a fuss
Walked across
Red velvet rug
Yellow tassels
On my neck
Ava's there
Ain't born yet

Her blue eyes
Never forget

Big corner lot
A brown house
Kind my dreams
Always been about

It turned red
Heart was black
No way I'm ever
Going back

On my own
A green house
To call my home

Met a man
With eyes blue
He promising
To stay true

Double rainbow
Let it last
No shame
My colored past

changed

You say I seem different
I'm not as you remember me
It occurs to me that I am in fact different
I'm so very different that I am unsure who I really am
Am I this girl that changed so much to appease someone else
that now I am screaming in technicolor or
Perhaps I am muted and distilled down to nothing
What am I
Who am I
I am floating in this nothingness and everythingness
I just want space to be whatever it is I am
Today
Tomorrow
Every day
Will my friends accept me
Will my lover accept me
Will I free me
What if I can't decide
What if I have decided
I am changing
I am forever changed
I can never be what I was
I never want to go back
There was a short time I thought I wanted to go back
To that place of blindness
I want to see all things now
I want to always be growing and changing
Shedding my old skin
Becoming a new version of myself
I see things
I feel things
I have never felt
I don't want to love blindly

I want to know
I need to know
I want to be accepted
I need to accept
You need to accept me
As what I am today
Can we still be friends if I am renewed
Would you accept me if I am ever evolving
I can't go back
I don't want to go back
Can we walk forward and see what there is over this hill
Will the wind smack our faces and send us backward
Will the wind be at our backs and caress us forward
Can you be open to whatever there is to come
I am stronger
I can do this alone
But I really don't want to
I want my friends here
Can you be supportive as I break through

made whole

Here I sit but on a tree
You are there in front of me
You glow as if burning from within
Your light so soothing I fall in
You roll me round inside your hand
I am heeding your demand
The branches you use to reinforce my joints
The sap you patch my broken points
The leaves a cloak to shield my skin
You have strengthened me yet again
Your fingers dig deep in your burning heart
You pull out a fiery flaming part
Gently folding creasing molding
You place it inside my heart now glowing
Deeply fully I breath in
I am made whole in your kiln

you are always there

When the day is long
And my patience runs thin
When my cup runneth over
And my joy is to the brim
You are always there

If my tire goes flat
You arrive with the spare
If my heart hurts
And I'm too numb to care
You are always there

When I recall all the
Happiness from yesterday
When I plan for tomorrow
Or I think of today
You are always there

grit

I have a friend who like me has had a hard life. And like me she also has a sibling. And like me, the sibling is vastly different. My friend and I took the road less traveled if you will. Thanks to a poet Robert Frost for this eloquent statement which is one of my favorite poems...but back to my point.

Our siblings traveled the path set forth by the tragedy of our shared experiences. For me, my family of origin is fraught with sexual, physical, and mental abuse sprinkled with addiction of drugs and alcohol, sex, and neglect. For her, not named so then permitted, domestic abuse of physical and mental harm, addiction and neglect.

Our siblings went down the modeled path. And really, why wouldn't they? But her and I? No, we did not go this path. We made our own way and later in our lives we made that way together. Being there for each other.

When I started counseling for the very first time as a grown-ass adult after my first breath-crushing PTSD episode in a perfectly safe environment, mind you...the counselor was amazed or perhaps wanted me to believe she was amazed that I was not an addict, a prostitute, an abuser, a murderer or at least a criminal.

Instead, I sat across from her at 30-plus years old that day a fully functioning (for the most part) college graduate with honors, successful professional, wife and mother who by the look of me had never had a hangnail let alone the basket full of tragedies I had just outlined for the first time aloud to a stranger.

The counselor told me she sees patients who are devastated after experiencing one divorce. Maybe they have an alcoholic parent. Maybe they are married to a workaholic. Maybe they have a special needs kid or lost their job and they are broken. She promised me all are broken, but some are just better at hiding it, like I had. But she said, you have a basket full or tragedies. Not just one, a basket. Of course you can't breath, can't sleep, can't eat. You are a miracle.

I remember talking with my friend after my counseling had begun and asking her why I wasn't a prostitute and she an addict. Without hesitation she stated that we had something our family didn't have or teach, we had a gift and the gift was grit. Looking backwards... at today... and ahead to tomorrow I am grateful to have grit and more importantly Her.

She is inspiring and it has been an honor to grow alongside her all these years. Thank you, my friend.

hope

What is this thing growing inside of me
It's been so long it's hard to see
Started as an ember hiding from the wind
Now it burns strongly yet again

It flickers and dances inside my heart
I can't describe exactly when did it start
Now it's wild and raging free
Like a wildfire bursting forth in me

Engulfing all with such great force
What power it has I have no choice
It takes hold of me, hope

girl

Who is that girl
So sure of herself
With all that strength but yet no wealth

Who does she think she is
No mask to hide her face
And that smile with my finger she traced

Where is she going
Without directions
No worry of possibly missing her connection

I have never seen her until today
But in the mirror I can't look away
Who is that girl if it not be me
Is she the one I was meant to be

hero

Have you ever met someone who helped you remember who you are or what dreams you may have let go along the way? I have. It can be a lover, a friend, a stranger, a villain perhaps. Whoever they may be, take a moment to thank them. For me, it is evermore complicated than just someone. For me it was two someones. One the villain of this story who taught me more about what I don't want than most anyone, and one the most handsome hero who showed me that I don't need permission to follow my dreams. I am thankful for them both. You see, a troll broke my heart. The villain. Honestly, I have come to learn I was naive. But back to the details...

This troll was veiled not by his design but by mine. He was never, not ever, what I had convinced myself he was. Transient really, the details. Specifics. The important thing to note is this illusion I created took great work to maintain. My toil took its toll. Thus the someone will be known as a troll. Blustery and warted, under a slimy bridge bursting forth from the shadows and stealing all your dreams as trolls are known to do. A dream can't be stolen, however, unless you first give it up. Truly. He never really stole anything from me I hadn't submissively discarded first. He is but a scavenger in the trash. I digress. So there it went, this dream and with it all of who I am. I was a ghost. Once you give your dream away to someone a sort of autopilot situation occurs. I took on his dreams. I smiled and nodded and continued to give up all these things that meant so much to me. Isn't that what a good partner does? No, it is absolutely not what a good partner does. But of course I didn't know that. How do people learn that before experiencing it? How do you teach that to your children? Okay, again I am off track...

It's a weird thing that occurs in a person who never backs down and always gets what they want at the expense of those around them. You might think this person must be incredibly happy and loving life, right? Wrong. They are miserable. You adjust to appease their misery, once again submitting all you desire to please them but it's a vicious spiraling abyss of displeasure. Nothing ever, and I mean ever, makes them happy. In my case, I spent my time in fidelity with my troll. All the while he was finding displeasure in others. I learned of his deeds and still I believed if I just submitted more of myself to him that he would be happy, we would be happy.

But then my hero came along. Brilliantly handsome and full of the deepest knowledge of me. All my wants and dreams, even as a child, my hero knew them. I became flooded with remembrance of all that I was. My hero then led me to my writings, pictures, and desires. Laid them out in front of me in the most glorious of epiphanies. Right there they lay bright and shining, making the puny troll and all his past deeds and renewed efforts to confuse me into submission seem juvenile. There was no balance to this scale in front of me. Clearly it was time for me to focus on my dreams. I was saved! I am whatever I want to be. No one ever stole anything from me I didn't first give away. Everything I needed was always right here. Now that I have learned this valuable lesson I can pursue my dreams. Permission? I don't need permission, I don't need help. I don't need a damn thing but my hero. What a glorious someone my hero is.

My hero is me and I am grateful.

forest bathing

Here it comes now
Rushing chemical release
Sweet as honey till it cease
The trees doth sing a lullaby
All you do is simply trod by
I knew of this treasure far before
Now in the newspaper pages three and four
All I feel is wild and true
The trees heal me and renew
The grass does fall as I stride by
But no matter, the roots are spry
There be a fungus in the tree
A weed, a branch, a bumbly bee
All content to completely ignore me
As I mosey now in the healing chemical
Which makes me cry ever grateful
Or I laugh at my mountain now trifle
A soft sob I attempt to stifle
Hikers really don't seem to mind
They notice the crying all the time
It is the trees healing us all
Take a moment and bathe in awe
They heal you and you heal me
Just go bathe there in the trees
If you don't believe me read page three

they know

A veil of soft wet leaves blankets the ground

Celebrating the end of life in a vibrant dance of color and surrender as they tumble to the ground

For now, shielding the grass from the assault to come

Unforgiving cold, and burning snow
They will fail however, the leaves
In their final effort to shield the grass

The dying wish, unrequited as the desire of the frosting snow outweighs the fickle leaf and its unending flirtation with the wind

Too soon they depart, the grass left betrayed

Slumber
Renewal

Does the grass know it will be reborn from seed and root
Does the tree know to hold water in the deepest part of its trunk
Do they talk to each other as they sway and bristle in the early morning cold

They do
They know

We must prepare for the great triumph of cessation in hibernation
So we may burst forth again even stronger in the months to come

Listen to their wisdom

seasons

I feel as though I am turning a page. I see on the horizon a glimpse of the answer to the question of what this season offers. I must give up this burden. I cannot control or ever know what someone else will do or say or feel. They could possibly show one thing or perhaps even my mind shows me something that isn't there. I must just go on. Fulfilling my needs, my desires, my lessons. My lesson is that I have no control. It is a lesson of faith. A lesson of blindness. Not the kind of blind faith I had before. I was naive. This faith feels like a choice. An educated choice. I make the choice to go forward. I choose to believe you, I choose to understand the risk and prepare my heart for a great romance or a great disappointment... But ultimately, I have made the choice. The season has shown its colors and I'm not as afraid. Her leaves are turning and they are brilliant. I must fix my eyes on the road ahead and be ever ready for any changes in the weather.

monster for dinner

There once was a snarling, clawing monster with fangs dripping bare
She lived in the closet or under the bed
She would come uninvited, in the thick of night
My heart would race
Belly grew tight
Many a sleepless night
She stole from me
Fear would fill each corner of my mind
Lost sleep, hours awake
Terror left, in her wake
This dance we had
Tiresome

One night, I turned the light off
Left the door and window ajar
Coaxing her out in the dead of night
She came
My heart was weary
I looked her in her ghostly face and...
Invited her to dinner Tuesday

She was unsure
Growling and concerned
How the table on her
I had suddenly turned
She agreed to a place and time
And arrived late but I paid it no mind
She broke a chair
Spilled her wine
Used her hands to eat and left a mess
But she felt it rude to return in the evening
Now that I had hosted her so graciously
So it went

If she would show unexpectedly, I would offer a better place and time
Eventually she showered and started arriving respectfully early
Learned to use a spoon and napkin
Even how to sip the wine
One day she offered to help with the dishes

Wouldn't you know, we have a standing appointment
She honors my boundaries and I understand the importance of the work she does
We have come a long way and discussed many a dark space in my mind
Now we just do it at an agreeable place and time
Me and my monster at the dinner table, Tuesdays, quarter to nine

do not forget

Take each step with the wonder you did your first and the wisdom it could be your last
Though there is a strangeness ahead, do not waiver
Hold your head high and give in to the newness of what is happening enough to be strange yourself
If you encounter darkness do not succumb to its devoid for you often get what you visualize
Instead, be unabashedly optimistic even to the moment cold and unforgiving dirt is thrown at your face for you are the mastermind of your destiny
Your destiny is love, and understanding that comes from the strength you gain in moments of weakness or vulnerability
Do not fear these parts of yourself or others
They are the truest you will ever know
Truth is strength and no amount of lies will ever change what is real
So do not lie, especially to yourself
Never forget this

ready yourself

You are gonna be okay
Be kind to yourself
Stop saying you're sorry when you don't mean it
And definitely stop saying it when you haven't done anything
wrong
Don't apologize for how you feel
Even when your feelings make things more complicated
Just allow yourself to feel
Acknowledge the feelings and then move forward
Don't sit in them long enough you become them
Laugh when its uncomfortable, laugh when it's funny
Just laugh, even if it's only in your mind for your own benefit
Listen more, God, this is the sauce here
I'm not just talking about life or work
Listen to the trees, listen to the hum of everything around you
Acknowledge the vibration of others and decide if you want
to allow it inside
You must make the choice
Stop allowing foreign things to just enter your world and your
mind
Make a conscious choice to hear them or pass them by
Success is on its way to you
Personally and professionally
All you do is ready yourself and your environment for the
Love you seek
The security you crave
The fulfillment you desire
It is charging toward you at an alarming rate
Ready yourself for the explosion of greatness
There will most likely be situations of toxicity you cannot
simply abandon
Whether it's a work situation, family, the ties that bind
Hold you to this angry pulse of unhappiness

First, make doubly sure you cannot simply leave
If you truly can't, and the situation is permanent, then you
need to seek help
If it's temporary, then let go
Remind yourself this is a blip
Note the season of learning you're in
Be grateful for the lessons you have already had
Think of how this will improve your inner self
Adapt to the moment but remember
You only control how you respond
Your thoughts and emotions are not in control
The situation is not in control
Just know your place in the season and let it run its course
Finally, love
Love those who do not deserve it, most especially
You can love them at a safe distance, quietly
But love them
Love those who deserve it
Love them so hard it takes their breath away
Love the ground which is always there to steady you
Love the people who love you and the people who hate and
the people you don't know
Love yourself and all the things within your delicate skin
You are magnificent

letter to self

Dearest Kerry Lynne,

It is my greatest hope this letter reaches you at the exact moment you require it. Without too much awkward foreshadowing I will just say, I know you. Born fatherless at a hospital in Lexington, Kentucky... This may seem unimportant but you will learn quickly, it isn't. Would your experiences have been much different if your father had been present and fully active in your life? I really don't know... But let's get back to it, shall we? Your mother was a rolling stone. By that I mean she was stoned, most of the time. Your aunt nearly adopted you because of your mother's bad choices and your father's absence. Once again, another moment where things may have been different. Your mother eventually stopped the adoption and took you back but she didn't stop abusing drugs and alcohol.

There is so much to cover. In your early years your greatest skill is adaptation. Your mother allows horrible people to sleep under her roof, which leads to a cascade of trauma with no escape. Physical abuse, sexual abuse, neglect. Horrid moments in time pierce your mind in the darkest caverns. Many of those memories mercifully hidden even now. Your mind clutched them away to protect you. What a glorious thing your mind is, Kerry. Don't ever lose sight of it. I digress. The physical abuse begets the sexual abuse because, well, at least the man isn't hitting you... and the sexual abuse begets the neglect because, well, now he isn't touching your mom, which makes her oddly jealous and distant... and so it goes. You become so good at adapting parts of yourself to survive the surroundings you begin to wonder who you are. Or maybe, you never felt comfortable enough to become whatever it is you had been destined to become. Nothing but hatred blooms in a war zone. Weeds perhaps. You are magnificently so much more than a weed.

By age 13 you have been abandoned by both parents, physically abused and sexually abused, neglected, arrested and abandoned again in a girls' juvenile home. Your mom comes back to save you, cigarettes and alcohol oozing from her pores. Odessa, your younger sister, is ecstatic to see mom strolling in through the cage doors of the girls' home after breaking her binder early. She just wanted her momma, too young to know she's the root of this shared evil. You, on the other hand, consider staying momentarily but realize you have no control. This feeling of having no control really comes to define you and your trauma responses as an adult.

~*~

Actually, this would be an ideal time to skip forward a bit... but I don't want to leave out the shooting. Just after your 13th birthday a man is shot by one of your mother's boyfriends in front of you. Literally, he is leaning over you through the passenger side window trying to punch the driver in a parked car while you struggle under his weight in the passenger seat. You hear a loud bang, which makes it impossible to hear anything else and then warm liquid is dripping down your chest and into your underwear. Blood—not your blood, by the grace of God. The man's blood. The cops come and sorta save the day. The cops. You have a love-hate relationship with them and more to come on that front… But their authority is not lost on you in these pivotal moments. They pluck you away from the toxic home with your toxic mom, brief reprieves throughout your life. But you begin to see them as saviors or father figures that don't try to punch you or fuck you. And in your twisted world that means something.

The man who shot the other… he slept in your mom's bed and you aborted his baby at age 15. Your mom paid for the abortion. It's actually a shocker you didn't get pregnant sooner. He had been fondling you since he moved in when you were barely 11 years old. Your beautiful baby's name is River. You cried and screamed out for your mom during the grotesque procedure and the doctor threatened to leave you there with "the fetus" dripping from your womb if you continued to scream and "scare the other patients." You shut the hell up—he was in charge after all—and he made that abundantly clear. You will eventually stop giving your power away to men with false authority. This I promise.

Continuing on, you have your share of relationships. Actually, since your virginity wasn't a consensual moment in time, you use sex to gain control or an edge early in interactions with men. You like sex and you like getting right down to it, which puts you in many unsettling situations. It takes longer than it should for you to realize using sex to gain control is the opposite of what actually happens. Luckily you are incredibly smart and adaptable, thanks to a life of war, and you manage to escape a few precarious situations unscathed. You have more lovers than you care to admit and decide you want something more. You need something more.

You meet a cop while selling a living-room suite and get married. He's a cop. You ignore many red flags, thinking back to those times when the cops always helped. You forget they are just human. You love him as deeply as he will allow, which isn't very deeply. But you took an oath before God and all the people you know. You feel secure in those words, too secure. You have a high tolerance for pain and suffering, clearly. He teaches you many lessons. You are gifted another baby and she is the most precious thing you have ever laid eyes on, held, grown. She is glorious. She is the only good thing from your marriage. It breaks you. You are more broken in the betrayal of your partner than all the other loss you have experienced. You feel weak to admit this because it's just betrayal. Just lies. But that's how it feels. The hurt is so much more than blood from your hymen, blood from another man, blood from an abortion. This hurt breaks the core of your identity up to then. The good wife doing all she could to try and make someone else happy all while barely holding herself together. Nearby, a beautiful adoring child with a life not at all like the one you lived, which was achingly purposeful. It was gone. It's like you died. And you did. You died.

Your rebirth is messy. Why wouldn't it be? You have never felt more alive though. You are living in this rawness and although it took a little while, you are relishing in your personal awareness of these growths and changes or maybe more realistically, a becoming of your destined self. This is who you are. You now believe the imperfections are what define people. Vulnerability and intimacy of the whole self is true love. The journey is marked with blood and tears. You are not done. But I am sure you are done hiding and definitely done with people who hide from you. The only authority left is God and the authority of self. No person, no shame, will ever control you again.

You have met someone. He is broken too and trying to show you parts of himself he hasn't shown to others before. This is helping you learn people are in different stages of their journey. Patience needs to be part of your relationships. Watch the majesty of learning happening around you, to those around you, to you, because of you. Notice and marinate in the growth. ...Those are the words I will leave you with.

Always and forever,
Kerry Lynne

P.S., I would have given you lottery numbers if money was important, but it isn't. I would have given you secrets if revealing them would give you more than fodder, but secrets are rife with shame and no one wins in shaming another, you absolutely know this to be true. I would have told you to avoid certain pathways or people, but the journey leads you to such a wonderful place full of wonderfully broken people and the tragedy of things turning out different, albeit easier on you, is too much to bear. So please, no matter when this reaches you... stay the course. Be strong, be weak, and know we are going to find a peace we never thought possible.

about the author

Kerry Lynne

Kerry Lynne, the author of *Fire Sale, Y'all*, lives in Noblesville, Indiana, with her adolescent daughter and grumpy fur baby. She returns to her home state of Kentucky often to visit family and hike the beautiful trails.

She is developing a follow-up collection, *Smell the Roses, Y'all: A Journey of Healing and Love in Poetry and Prose*, which continues her story of healing and rebuilding trust. Additionally, she is working on a fictionalized autobiography that delves deeper into her experiences with homelessness, abuse, and PTSD.

Connect with Kerry

If you would like to connect with the author, you can find her here:

Email: home@whoiskerrylynne.com
Website: www.whoiskerrylynne.com
Social Media:
www.youtube.com/@whoisKerryLynne
www.facebook.com/profile.php?id=61558040773570
www.instagram.com/whoiskerrylynne/